Bert and the

WRITTEN BY VIVIAN FR...

ILLUSTRATED BY ED BOXALL

SWAG

WALKER BOOKS
AND SUBSIDIARIES
LONDON · BOSTON · SYDNEY · AUCKLAND

Chapter One

Police Constable
Bert Butts liked
   1. skipping ...

   2. fluffy
      kittens ...

   3. writing
      poems.

Most of all he liked Wonderful
Police Constable Marigold Rose.

3. catching burglars!

She did NOT like Bert Butts.

When she saw him skipping
along the road she sniggered.

When she saw him stroke
a kitten she stuck her nose
in the air.

When Bert wrote a poem for the *Police Journal* she laughed.

It was not a nice friendly laugh.
It was a loud and scornful laugh.

Chapter Two

One day two notices were pinned
up on the police noticeboard.
Here they are:

£100 REWARD!!!!
Wanted behind bars –
Whiskers Wheeler, Cat Burglar

Come to the

Party

at

Parkside Police Station

on

June 30th
at 4.00p.m.

Come with a friend

Marigold read the reward notice. She was very excited. Perhaps she could catch the cat burglar and win the reward? Then she could buy herself an even fiercer dog.

Bert read the invitation.
He was very excited indeed.
Perhaps he could ask Marigold
to go to the party with him?
He went to find her.

"Marigold," Bert said shyly,
"will you go to the party with me?"
Marigold snorted. It was a loud
and scornful snort.

What a wimp!

"I'll go to the party with you IF you
catch the cat burglar!" she said.

But I'm going to
catch him myself!

Then she laughed and walked
away with her nose in the air.

Bert sighed, and went home
to write a poem.

Oh Marigold
You are very cold
Like a block of ice
And sometimes you are
not very nice
To me
But I still love you.

Chapter Three

Bert woke up early the next day.
He began to think very hard.
1. If I catch the cat burglar Marigold
will go to the party with me …

2. AND if I catch the cat burglar
I'll win the £100 reward …

3. SO it would be a very good thing indeed to catch the cat burglar.

Bert counted the days till the party.

Seven days seemed
like a long time.

Bert decided to make a plan.

Sunday:
Have a rest so I'm not tired on Monday

Monday:
Look for clues

Tuesday:
Look for more clues

Wednesday:
Catch Whiskers Wheeler the cat burglar

Thursday:
Collect reward

Friday:
Ask Marigold to go to the party

Saturday:
Go to the party with Marigold
and live Happily Ever After

It seemed like a very good plan.
Bert smiled happily and went
to make himself a cup of tea.

Chapter Four

On Sunday Bert's plan worked
very well.

On Monday he went to look for
clues. He found lots of footprints,
but none of them belonged to
Whiskers Wheeler.

On Tuesday he went to look for more clues. He found more footprints, but still none of them belonged to Whiskers Wheeler.

On Wednesday Bert felt gloomy.
Would he ever catch the cat
burglar?
He went to look for more clues –
and he saw...

SOMEONE HIDING BEHIND A BUSH!
Bert rushed to arrest them.

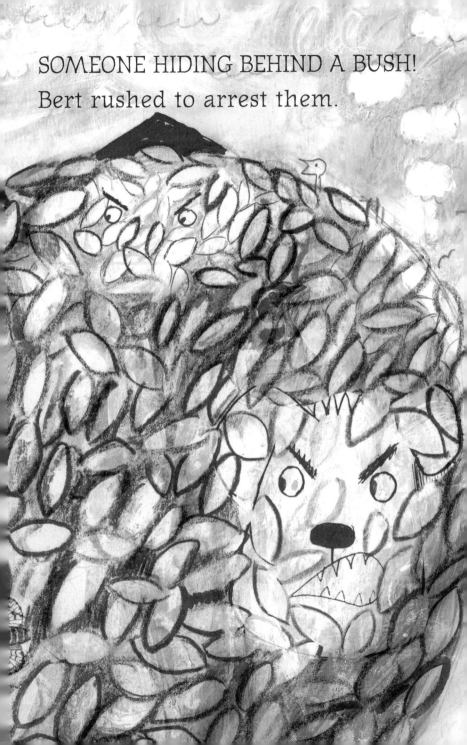

"GO AWAY!" said WPC Marigold Rose crossly. "Whiskers is MY burglar and I'M going to catch him!"

Bert felt even gloomier
as he walked slowly home.

That night Bert had a fantastic idea.

Whiskers Wheeler is a CAT burglar.
So — if I dress up as a cat,
whiskers wheeler will catch ME!
And then I can catch HIM!

It was such a fantastic idea that Bert jumped out of bed. In no time at all he was dressed as a cat and skipping down the road.

I'm off to catch Whiskers Wheeler Because he is a cat stealer!

"Meeow!" Bert called. "Meeow!"
Up and down and round
the town he went.

All the cats in all the houses
heard Bert. They hurried outside
and followed along behind him.

"Go away, cats!" said Bert, but the cats didn't go away. More and more came to follow him.

Bert skipped faster ...
and faster ...
down the road ...
round a corner ...

CRASH!

"MARIGOLD!" gasped Bert. "You're dressed as a mouse!"

"BERT!" gasped WPC Marigold Rose. "You're dressed as a cat!"

"MY HEAD!" moaned the whiskery man in between them. "IT HURTS!"

Whatever's going on?

"I thought if I dressed as a cat then a cat burglar would catch me," said Bert.

"I thought if I dressed as a mouse a cat burglar would catch ME," said Marigold.

The whiskery man sighed loudly.
"Cat burglars don't catch cats,"
he said.
"Oh," said Bert.
"And cat burglars don't catch
mice either," said the man.
"Oh," said Marigold.
"No," said the man. "They're
called cat burglars because they
JUMP like a cat."

And he jumped up and away
onto a wall...

All the little cats meeowed so loudly that Whiskers Wheeler the cat burglar wobbled ...

and the big cats got in his way so he slipped and fell ...

PLOP! into Bert and Marigold's
arms.

"GOTCHA!"
they shouted.

They're called
cat burglars because
it's cats that
catch them!

Chapter Five

Bert and Marigold shared
the reward.
Bert bought a fluffy dog
for Marigold.

Marigold bought a
fierce kitten for Bert.

They went to the police party together.

Did they live happily
ever after?
What do you think?

Thank you for reading my stor-y
There isn't any more-y
Because this is the end
Love from your friend
Bert.

x x x

For Sarah and Bayo
with kisses
V. F.

For Sammy and Rachel
E. B.

First published 2004 by Walker Books Ltd
87 Vauxhall Walk, London SE11 5HJ

2 4 6 8 10 9 7 5 3

Text © 2004 Vivian French
Illustrations © 2004 Ed Boxall

The right of Vivian French and Ed Boxall to be identified
as author and illustrator respectively of this work has
been asserted by them in accordance with the
Copyright, Designs and Patents Act 1988

This book has been typeset in Journal Text

Handlettering by Ed Boxall

Printed in China

British Library Cataloguing in Publication Data:
a catalogue record for this book
is available from the British Library

ISBN 1-84428-605-3

www.walkerbooks.co.uk